WILD MAGIC

LEGEND OF THE BLACK LION

WILD MAGIC

MAGIC

LEGEND OF THE BLACK LION

ABJOLA BELLO

ILLUSTRATED BY EMMA McCANN

SIMON & SCHUSTER

London New York Amsterdam/Antwerp Sydney/Melbourne Toronto New Delhi

First published in Great Britain in 2025 by Simon & Schuster UK Ltd

1 3 5 7 9 10 8 6 4 2

Simon & Schuster UK Ltd
1st Floor, 222 Gray's Inn Road
London WC1X 8HB

www.simonandschuster.co.uk
www.simonandschuster.com.au
www.simonandschuster.co.in

Simon & Schuster Australia, Sydney
Simon & Schuster India, New Delhi

The authorised representative in the EEA is Simon & Schuster
Netherlands BV, Herculesplein 96, 3584 AA Utrecht, Netherlands.
info@simonandschuster.nl

A CIP catalogue record for this book is available
from the British Library.

PB ISBN 978-1-3985-2048-6
eBook ISBN 978-1-3985-2050-9
eAudio ISBN 978-1-3985-2049-3

Typeset in the UK by Sorrel Packham

Printed and Bound in the UK using
100% Renewable Electricity at CPI Group (UK) Ltd

To my magical nephew, Akorede.

May you continue to shine bright x

CHAPTER ONE
The Next Big Adventure

Misha lay on the sofa and wrapped her long braids into two buns on the top of her head. It was the first day of the

summer holidays. She flipped through her comic book, ignoring the grey Bengal cat with green eyes that was purring next to her.

'One second, Fergie,' she said.

Fergie rubbed his head against her arm and Misha laughed. 'I'll get you a snack. Let me just finish this part, okay?'

The cat **purred** loudly.

'I know, you told me yesterday. I'll get you the white fish treat this time.'

Fergie jumped from the sofa and walked over to the Staffordshire Bull Terrier called Blue, who was curled up asleep in her bed, her red plastic balls by her feet. Fergie pushed himself onto the bed beside her. Misha shook her head, smiling. Fergie had said Blue's bed was comfier than his, and luckily Blue didn't mind sharing as long as her toys weren't moved.

The other grey cat, identical to Fergie, **MEOWED** loudly from the chair across the room.

Misha ignored it and the cat meowed again even **louder** as if he wanted all of the neighbours to hear.

'Shh!' Misha said. 'And, no, it's not my problem that you're bored.' Loud footsteps pounded down the stairs and Misha looked at the closed door. `Quick, Ziggy!'

The grey cat **LEAPED** into the air and when it landed, in its place was her eight-year-old twin brother with his curly high-top haircut. Ziggy quickly sat on a chair and flicked on the TV, trying to act like he'd been a human all along.

'Ziggy?' Misha said, and when he looked at her, she pointed to her nose.

Ziggy touched his own nose and felt the **whiskers**. He shook his head and they disappeared just as the living-room door opened.

'Hi, Dad,' Misha and Ziggy said in unison.

'JINX!' Misha said, like they always did when they spoke at the same time. Which happened a lot – it was a **twin thing**.

'Ah, man,' Ziggy groaned.

'You know the rules,' Misha responded, and she mimed zipping her

lips. Ziggy pouted and crossed his arms over his chest.

'Hi, kids,' Dad said. He was a tall, slim, dark-skinned man with a neatly trimmed black beard and black-framed glasses. 'How's the comic, Misha?'

'It's really good! It's about a girl whose big sister is a superhero.'

'Are you reading anything fun, Ziggy?' Dad asked, and Ziggy pointed at his mouth.

'I jinxed him. *That means he can't talk,*' Misha said proudly.

Dad laughed. 'Well, do you mind un-jinxing him so he can answer me?'

Misha sighed. 'I guess.' She knocked her knuckles on the wooden table, like they always did when they had to reverse a jinx, and Ziggy **WHOOPED**

loudly as if he had been silenced for days.

'It's the summer holidays, Dad! I'm not doing any reading for the next six weeks!' Ziggy said. Dad frowned, but as he was about to respond, Ziggy shouted, **'DAD, IT'S YOU!'** Ziggy excitedly turned up the volume on the TV and the familiar theme song of Dad's wildlife show filled the room.

Misha closed her comic book and sat up. The twins loved watching their dad on TV. He was a wildlife TV presenter and his job took him all over the world, where he got to see the most amazing animals up close and personal, from **BOISTEROUS BABOONS** to **CHEEKY CHEETAHS**. But sometimes Dad and the film crew couldn't find the animals they were searching for – Dad always says, *'There are no rules in the wild!'* – and so the big bosses of the TV channel would ask him to travel to the same country again to try to find them. This meant that Misha and Ziggy wouldn't see their dad for weeks on end.

But the twins knew if they were with Dad, they could help him find the animals he was looking for. Because the twins had **special powers**. Gifts that they had inherited from their mum when they turned six years old. **MISHA COULD TALK TO ANIMALS**, and **Ziggy could shapeshift into them**. The problem was, Dad didn't know about their powers, or Mum's. Grandma Yinka had warned Misha and Ziggy to keep their powers a secret because when their mum was a teenager, people from the Nigerian village she grew up in were scared of her when they found out about her gifts. It was better to be safe than sorry.

But their mum seemed to prefer being around animals than humans. Whenever she would take the twins on trips to the park or the cinema, she would speak to the birds flying above them in the sky or shapeshift into a squirrel they saw on the street. Mum made Misha and Ziggy keep this a secret, which they did because their mum's powers made her **cool!** Then, one day, just after their eighth birthday, the twins came home and Mum had vanished. They found the shedded skin of a chameleon on their Mum's favourite chair and knew she had left to live in her animal form. They both wondered if Dad would ever find her in the wild on one of his many film trips, and they hoped that they would see her again. But they tried not to miss her too much because they still had their dad, and he was the best.

So, every time Dad went on his next trip, the twins were left behind at their grandparents' house. Not their cool Grandma Yinka, who lived in a hut in the deep Nigerian forest, casting **magical spells**. It would be amazing to be around someone who they didn't have to hide their powers from.

No. They had to stay with Grandma Joy and

Grandpa Tunde, Dad's parents. Grandma Joy and
Grandpa Tunde lived across the road from Misha
and Ziggy's house and were *so* strict. Grandpa Tunde
made Misha and Ziggy do their homework during
the school holidays! Plus, Grandma Joy **HATED**
animals! She always had her broom ready to swipe

at any animals that came close to her house. It was no fun for the twins, though. Misha loved it when animals came to visit – she finally had someone else to talk to other than her brother. But when Grandma Joy shooed them away, Misha sometimes felt lonely. And Ziggy was always at risk of one of Grandma Joy's broom swipes when he was in animal form. One time, Grandma Joy hit him when he was with a group of badgers, sitting on her dining table and nibbling apples, pears and plums from the fruit bowl.

Now that Dad was about to go on another work trip, this meant staying with Grandma Joy and Grandpa Tunde once again.

'Do you think you're going somewhere hot or cold on your next adventure?' Ziggy asked.

Dad put a finger to his chin. 'I think hot.

Hopefully, with a beach and clear-blue water, so I can see all the tropical fish.'

'Why can't we go?' Misha moaned for the hundredth time.

The beach sounded great, but really Misha wanted to speak to the wild animals. She only got the chance to speak to her pets, the neighbours' rabbits, and Ziggy, when he transformed into random animals. She dreamed of being up close to a leopard or a dolphin and hearing their stories. Plus, she could wipe the smug smile off Cassie Evans, a girl in her class who always boasted about her amazing summer holidays to every exotic place imaginable. Cassie found it hilarious that their dad travelled the world, but the twins were stuck in London.

Ziggy was desperate to travel with Dad because

he wanted to see what new animals he could shapeshift into. With his powers, he could only transform into the animal that he was physically close to in real life, but once he had done it the first time, he could do it again at his command. So far, he only shapeshifted into small- and medium-sized animals that he usually saw in London. If he were to travel to all the wild places with Dad, imagine what animals he could transform into? Could his power make him as **BIG AS A WHALE?** As **TALL AS A GIRAFFE?** Maybe he could become a shark and swim up behind Misha when she was playing in the ocean and make her jump.

The thought made Ziggy **laugh out loud**. Misha and Dad looked at him and he quickly put his hand over his mouth to control himself.

Dad's phone rang in his hand. 'That's the TV producers now. I'll just be in my office and then we'll go out for dinner.'

As soon as their dad left, the twins walked over to the globe that sat beside the bookshelf. Dad had bought it for them so they could always see where he was. Ziggy spun it so fast that it tilted even more to the side. Misha quickly straightened it up before it fell.

'Okay, I bet you *two cinnamon pretzels* that he's going to India,' Ziggy said, pointing at the globe. 'They have loads of cool animals like tigers, elephants and the Indian cobra!'

'Hmmm maybe,' Misha said, turning the globe more gently. 'I bet you **THREE CHOCOLATE-CHIP COOKIES** that he's going to Australia. He can see the kangaroos, koalas and crocodiles!'

15

'If you could speak to any animal, which one would you pick?' Ziggy asked.

'There are so many! Maybe a lion? I would love to hear what it's like to be the king of the jungle. What animal would you want to shapeshift into?'

Ziggy didn't think she would appreciate his shark fantasy, but suddenly that was all he could think about!

'Oh, anything really,' he mumbled.

Before Misha could question Ziggy further, the familiar footsteps of Dad raced up the stairs. He opened the door with a massive smile on his face. 'Kids, I'm going to **ETHIOPIA!'**

CHAPTER TWO
The Legendary Black Lion

There was a moment of silence. Dad looked excitedly at the twins.

'Where's Ethiopia?' Ziggy asked.

'It's in **Africa**, isn't it, Dad?' Misha asked.

'That's right. Let me show you.' Dad joined them at the globe and bent down so he was at eye level with it. He spun it so Africa was facing them. 'So,

we come from Nigeria, which is in West Africa, but **Ethiopia is in East Africa.** Dad pointed to Ethiopia, which was beside Sudan and Kenya.

'What's in Ethiopia?' Misha asked.

Dad's eyes widened. **'The legendary black lion.'**

Misha and Ziggy looked at each other with the same wide eyes.

'The black lion has only been seen in Ethiopia, and we finally located it. I'll be travelling there next week.' Dad rubbed his hands together and smiled. 'It's going to be amazing.'

A black lion? Misha and Ziggy had never heard of it before, but it was definitely something they wished they could see in person too. It just wasn't fair!

'I'll take loads of pictures,' Dad promised when he saw the sad looks on their faces. 'Come on, guys, you're going to have loads of fun at your grandparents'. Look, let's call them now!'

Before they could object, Dad whipped out his phone to video-call Grandma Joy and Grandpa Tunde. 'Come on, scoot in, Zig,' he said, and Ziggy reluctantly joined his dad and sister.

But when Grandma Joy answered the video call, they didn't see her cream-coloured floral living room, but instead a sparkling blue ocean.

Dad frowned. 'Mum? I can't see you?'

The video went dark and then Grandma Joy appeared with sunglasses on.

'What in the world?' Dad said. 'Where are you?'

'The Caribbean!' Grandma Joy said. 'Oh, hello,

babies.' She waved at Misha and Ziggy, who waved back.

Dad's frown went even deeper. 'The Caribbean? Why?'

'I'm on my cruise! Don't you remember? Look, I'm here with your dad. Say hello, Tunde.'

Grandma Joy turned the camera and Grandpa Tunde was lying on a sun lounger with his hands clasped on his belly, fast asleep.

'Mum!' Dad said, his voice rising. 'When are you back?'

'In a month,' Grandma Joy sang.

'*A month?*' Ziggy mouthed to Misha.

Misha didn't want to get too excited, but if Grandma Joy and Grandpa Tunde were away on holiday, then they couldn't stay with them. Could they be meeting the black lion after all?

'You know I have to travel next week for filming. I just found out that I'm going to Ethiopia. You're meant to be watching the kids!'

'Oh, I'm sorry, darling,' Grandma Joy said, taking a sip of her drink, not looking sorry at all. 'I got the dates mixed up. Can't you take them with you?'

'Take them with me? Mum, you need to come back! Mum? Mum?'

The video froze. Dad tapped his phone screen impatiently, but Grandma Joy and her big smile just stared back at them.

Misha and Ziggy **FIST-BUMPED** each other behind their dad's back. They were going to Ethiopia!

As soon as he hung up the video call, Dad called everyone he knew and asked if they could look after Misha and Ziggy, including their neighbour Esther, who lived two doors down and was definitely older than Grandma Yinka and Grandma Joy combined! Misha and Ziggy didn't want to stay with her because her house was *very* **boring!** She almost said yes, until she remembered Misha and Ziggy's cat, Fergie, and dog, Blue, who she would also have to look after but couldn't because she had terrible allergies to animal fur.

Finally admitting defeat, Dad told the twins they would be joining him. Dad's work trips usually occurred during the school term, so Misha and Ziggy had plenty to do to keep them occupied when he was away. This time, his work trip was in the summer holidays, and they had been extra disappointed that they wouldn't get to spend time with him. But not any more! They couldn't wait to get on the plane, arrive in Ethiopia, see all the amazing animals and share the best experiences with Dad. What a way to spend their summer holidays!

That will definitely beat Cassie Evans's summer vacation, Misha thought, with a sly grin.

'There will be ground rules,' Dad said sternly. 'You will have a chaperone at all times. No running off, no being on the film set and no being alone around the animals. They are wild and it will be very dangerous.'

No alone time with the wild animals? Misha huffed. How was she supposed to speak to them? That was a big reason why she wanted to go.

'When you say, no wild animals, do you really mean, *no* wild animals?' Ziggy asked, and Dad glared at him.

'I'm serious. This is a work trip and you both need to be on your best behaviour. I know you'll get excited seeing the animals, but you cannot wander and you cannot be alone. Got it?'

'Yes, Dad,' the twins mumbled.

But once their dad's back was turned, they winked at each other. There was no way they were going to miss the black lion. Not in a **BAZILLION** years!

CHAPTER THREE
Welcome to Ethiopia

Finally, the day was here! The twins had spent the week learning all about the animals in Ethiopia, from the yellow-fronted parrot to the Ethiopian wolf. Dad promised to take them to the Simien Mountains National Park, where they would hopefully see a leopard. Dad told them all about the black lion, which was also known as the **Abyssinian lion**. They are very rare and so many people fear they will become extinct in the future. The black lion is known for the dark fur on its mane, which could be because of a genetic mutation. Misha and Ziggy thought that its black mane was like its superpower, so maybe they were more like this awesome animal than they first thought!

On the plane, Ziggy couldn't contain himself. He hadn't been on one since they'd flown to Nigeria three years earlier. He kept his eyes glued to the window, looking at the sky and imagining all the birds he could shapeshift into. Nothing like the ones he'd seen in his garden, which he had transformed into so many times. Ziggy couldn't wait to see the variety of birds in Ethiopia, and many of them had the coolest names like sombre rock chat and yellow-throated seedeater. Much more exciting than a pigeon or a seagull.

Dad had told them that Ethiopia had a different calendar, so was eight years behind the rest of the world. Dad said this is because it calculates the birth year of Jesus Christ differently to the Western calendar. The twins couldn't believe that they were **FLYING INTO THE PAST!**

Almost eight hours later, Misha, Ziggy and Dad landed in Ethiopia. As soon as they got off the plane, they immediately started sweating. It was so hot, like they were being baked in an oven! As they

walked through the airport with all their luggage, a very tall Black man with long plaits down his back and a camera hanging from his shoulder shouted, **'DAYO! WELCOME TO ETHIOPIA!'**

Dad waved at him. 'That's Carter and the film crew,' he explained to the twins, indicating the group of people standing behind Carter. 'Come and say hello.'

Dad introduced them properly to Carter, who

was the cameraman; Lexi, a bubbly mixed-race lady with very curly brown hair and a friendly face, who was the director; and Ed, a stocky white man with freckles across his cheeks, who was the producer.

As they left the airport, they all got into a massive car with air conditioning and headed towards their new home. Misha and Ziggy looked at each other and grinned from ear to ear. They were actually in Ethiopia!

During the car ride, the city flew by, and soon they were surrounded by fields and mountains. Ziggy pressed his face to the window, hoping to catch a glimpse of any wild animals. He looked up and saw what appeared to be a group of deer standing on the mountain.

'They're called mountain nyala,' Dad said. He pointed to one that had a grey coat. 'That one is a male. You can tell because only the males have horns.'

'Do they ever come down to the lower ground?' Misha asked, following their gaze.

'They're quite shy around humans,' Dad explained.

Misha and Ziggy glanced at each other, both thinking the same thing: *They* wouldn't be scared of them.

They were now driving through the trees and it felt like they were surrounded by them for ages. Finally, the car stopped. They had arrived at their new home. It was the **COOLEST TREEHOUSE** Misha and Ziggy had ever seen. It was hidden deep in the

bushes and was two storeys high, with a wooden veranda and a windy, uneven staircase. At the very top, through the gaps in the trees, they had a perfect view of the glistening waterhole.

'**Whoa,**' Ziggy said, marvelling at the treehouse.

'This is amazing, Dad,' Misha said. 'I thought we would be camping.'

'Camping with wild animals wouldn't be safe for you both,' Dad explained, settling their suitcases on the floor. 'We'll sleep upstairs, and the film crew will sleep downstairs. Usually, we stay with the locals, but we need somewhere close to where the black lion has been seen. You two will stay here the whole time. There will be a few days when we will be filming all night, so me and the film crew will camp then.'

'Can't we come?' Ziggy asked.

Dad huffed. 'We already spoke about this, Zig. You're not allowed on the film set. That was one of my rules, remember? Now, why don't the both of you go and find a room to stay in and start to unpack, okay?'

The twins reluctantly went upstairs.

'I can't believe Dad is being serious about these rules,' Misha said, unzipping her suitcase which spilled out clothes onto the floor. 'What are we going to do?'

Ziggy didn't respond. He had a plan, but he knew if he told Misha, she would refuse to help him. Ziggy was going to see the animals, and no one was going to stop him.

'Kids, can you come downstairs, please?' Dad called, and the twins met him in the living room. 'The film crew and I have to meet our contact who has been keeping track of the black lion for us before we arrived, so I have to leave you both earlier than I expected. I'm sorry.' Dad kissed them both on the forehead. 'Let me introduce you to Hanna.'

Hanna was tall with glowing brown skin and bouncy, curly hair. 'Hello, Misha and Ziggy. Nice to meet you both.'

'Hi,' the twins said at the same time, and Ziggy immediately shouted, **'JINX!'**

Misha rolled her eyes and crossed her arms.

Dad smiled and shook his head. 'Kids, Hanna will look after you whenever I have to work during our trip. Please be on your best behaviour and remember to follow the rules. If you don't, I will be very disappointed.'

'They'll be in safe hands with me, Mr Asotun,' Hanna said with a wide smile.

As their dad and Hanna continued to talk, Ziggy looked out of the window where there was a small orange-and-white bird with a blue-and-black face sitting on the windowsill. It was a superb starling. It was one of the cool names that stood out to him during his and Misha's research. The colours were even more vibrant in real life. Misha followed his gaze and she hit him on the arm.

'OW!' he hissed, holding his arm protectively.

Misha pointed to her mouth and Ziggy reluctantly knocked on the wooden table.

'I know what you're thinking,' she whispered so Dad and Hanna couldn't hear. 'Don't you dare leave me here.'

Ziggy's eyes didn't leave the bird. 'I'll follow Dad and see where they go,' he whispered back. 'Then, when the coast is clear, we'll go ourselves. Cover for me.'

Misha stalled for a little bit and then gave in. 'Hanna, can you give me a tour of the treehouse? We've never stayed in one before,' Misha asked.

'Sure.' Hanna smiled brightly. 'Are you coming, Ziggy?'

Ziggy put his hand on his stomach. 'I need to go toilet.'

36

Dad waved at them as all the film crew filed out of the house. Hanna turned around to walk towards the back of the treehouse and, with only Misha watching him, Ziggy's face started to **SHRINK** and blue and black feathers **SPROUTED** from his skin. It almost looked like someone had **SQUEEZED** his body as he got **smaller and smaller**. His brown skin transformed into blue, orange and white feathers. His usually dark eyes were now white with a small black dot in the centre. Ziggy **flapped his wings** and hovered in the air, winking at Misha before he flew out of the door, just before Dad closed it behind him.

Now to find the black lion!

The journey following Dad's jeep was longer than Ziggy had expected. When Ziggy finally stopped, he had reached the waterhole. From their bedroom window, it had looked much closer, but there was a hidden road through the tall blades of grass and overgrown trees that had tricked the eye. Ziggy did his best to remember the route he had taken so that he could tell Misha.

Ziggy stopped a few metres away from Dad and

the film crew. An old man in a beige sun hat waved at them. Dad greeted him, and Ziggy followed quietly and closely behind, making sure he didn't look suspicious. As he passed the trees, he had a better view of the waterhole. Right now, it was empty.

'You must be Kemal.' Dad and Kemal shook hands. 'I'm Dayo Asotun. Thank you so much for meeting with us. We're so excited to see the black lion. This is Lexi, Ed and Carter, who will be filming the documentary with me.'

Kemal smiled and greeted the film crew before he took off his hat and looked at the floor. 'I'm sorry, but I have bad news.'

'*Bad news?*' Dad frowned.

'Yes. I have been keeping track of the black lion

for you all,' Kemal explained. 'But it's been four days and I haven't seen him. I know lions can go days without any water, but that's only if there isn't a water source. There are many here and **HE HASN'T APPEARED.'**

Ziggy gasped loudly, but it sounded like a **chirp**. Thankfully the grasslands were full of various animal noises, so no one paid him any attention.

Kemal stepped closer towards Dad and the film crew and said, 'Which is why I think something **bad** has happened to him.'

CHAPTER FOUR
How to Find a Lion

'Something bad?' Dad said. 'What do you think has happened to him?'

Kemal pointed to the green mountains behind him. 'Maybe he has moved on to the highlands and started his own pride.' Kemal sighed heavily. 'Or he may have been caught by poachers.'

'POACHERS?' Dad gasped, and Lexi, Ed and Carter shared the same fearful expressions.

Kemal continued, 'There are rumours that

poachers have been seen in the area. *The black lion is very rare and at the top of their catch-list.'*

'How can we know for certain what has happened to him?' Dad asked.

'We'll have to keep searching,' Carter said. 'We are lucky that Kemal was able to track him for as long as he did.'

Kemal smiled at Carter in gratitude.

'Kemal, if you can show us where you already searched, that would be helpful,' Lexi said. 'We can look again, just to be sure.'

'Of course,' Kemal replied.

'We'll do whatever it takes to find him,' Dad said reassuringly.

Don't worry, Dad. Me and Misha will help too, Ziggy thought.

Back at the treehouse, Dad and the film crew were downstairs in the living room discussing new plans to find the black lion, while Misha and Ziggy sat down for lunch on the veranda. Hanna placed injera – a pancake-like flatbread – a chickpea stew

called shiro and a cubed-beef dish called tibs on the table, then went back inside. Ziggy filled Misha in on the news and Misha felt so bad for Dad. She knew how important it was for him to get footage of the black lion.

'Are you sure you didn't see anything when you were at the waterhole?' Misha asked.

Ziggy shook his head. His cheeks were full as he stuffed his face with injera and tibs.

'**The black lion hasn't been seen in four days.** We should go to the waterhole tonight and see if we can find any clues. Maybe the animals can tell us something?' Misha suggested.

Ziggy swallowed his food. 'That's a good idea, but *how* are we going to get out without anyone noticing?'

Misha drummed her fingers on the wooden table. She had no clue.

Hanna came back out with a jug full of orange

juice. She frowned when she noticed Misha's untouched food. 'Come on, eat up. I've got a great film to watch later.'

Misha wanted to think, not eat. But because Hanna was watching her, Misha scooped up injera and shiro with her hands and shoved it into her mouth. Hanna sat down, satisfied.

Eventually, Dad joined them on the veranda. Below, Lexi, Ed and Carter waved goodbye as they left the treehouse to explore the neighbourhood. Dad could barely smile as he sat next to Misha, Ziggy and Hanna at the table.

'Is everything okay, Dad?' Ziggy asked.

Their dad took off his glasses and rubbed his eyes. 'The film crew and I had some problems today, but I'm sure we can sort it out. We're leaving early tomorrow morning to look for the black lion, so Hanna will take you to the Simien Mountains National Park.'

'But you promised to take us!' Misha protested. The Simien Mountains National Park was full of the most amazing animals, including some **endangered species**, and Dad would have been able to talk about every single one of them. She'd been so excited to go with him and Ziggy.

Dad hesitated. 'I did want to come,' he said slowly. He looked disappointed at the possibility of missing out on visiting the Simien Mountains National Park.

'No problem, Mr Asotun,' Hanna said. 'I can take them to Mercato Market instead. It's lots of fun and will keep the twins entertained. We can stay there all day.'

'*All day*,' Ziggy mouthed to Misha. He didn't

want to go to a market. **HE WANTED TO HANG OUT WITH THE ANIMALS!**

'I was wondering if we could see the waterhole,' Misha said quickly, and everyone looked at her. 'I've wanted to see it since we got here and I don't think I can wait.'

'Actually, there is a tourist bus that visits the waterhole and can pick us up from here,' Hanna said. 'There's also a tourist guide to make sure we don't get too close to the wild animals, so the kids can take pictures of them from afar. It's very safe, Mr Asotun. We can go in the morning if you want?' She smiled at Misha and Ziggy, who couldn't help but smile back. Hanna had no idea how much she was helping them.

'I'd feel better if I was with you,' Dad said.

'**Please,**' Misha and Ziggy begged with their

49

hands clasped as if praying.

'We'll be on our best behaviour,' Ziggy added.

Misha tried hard not to chuckle. Ziggy was rarely on his best behaviour. Dad must have been thinking the same thing, because he was looking at Ziggy with his eyes narrowed as if trying to read his mind to see what mischievous act he was thinking of. Ziggy put on his best *I am so loveable* expression, with his eyes wide and pleading.

Dad sighed. 'Fine. Hanna, I've told you the ground rules that Misha and Ziggy know they *must* follow at all times. And, kids, I expect you to be *perfect* for Hanna, okay?'

'Yes, Dad,' the twins chorused.

Misha and Ziggy **FIST-BUMPED** each other under the table.

CHAPTER FIVE
Off to the Waterhole

The next morning, Dad was ready to set out bright and early, giving the twins a quick kiss on the forehead and reminding them to be good. He looked at Ziggy the entire time. He was going to meet the film crew to work on their new plan for how to find the black lion.

The twins quickly dressed in shorts and T-shirts and headed down to the kitchen for breakfast, where Hanna placed a plate of fatira on the table. 'Here you go.'

Misha tried one first. 'Mmm, this is so good,' she said, and Hanna smiled. It was a pastry filled with scrambled eggs and honey.

'Wow!' Ziggy said, wiping pastry crust from his mouth. This was the tastiest thing he had ever eaten. Ziggy quickly ate four more until Misha moved the plate away.

'Save some for Hanna, greedy!'

Ziggy huffed and crossed his arms over his chest.

Hanna joined them and grabbed a fatira. 'These are my favourite!'

Misha gave Ziggy a knowing look.

'Are you guys excited to see some animals at the waterhole this morning?' Hanna asked.

'Yes! What kind of animals will we see?' Misha asked.

'Oh, zebras, warthogs. You might even see elephants.'

'**Elephants!**' Ziggy gasped. That would definitely be the **biggest animal** he had ever *shapeshifted into!*

'What about the black lion?' Misha asked.

Hanna frowned. 'I have heard rumours about sightings of the black lion and I know that's why your dad's here, but I haven't actually seen it. Maybe today will be our lucky day.'

'I hope so,' Misha muttered.

Once they had all finished eating breakfast and they'd each put a bottle of ice-cold water and wrapped-up fatiras in their waist bags, the tourist truck arrived to pick them up. Misha wished they could have walked down to the waterhole so she could take in the scenery and speak to any animals along the way, but it was boiling hot with very little breeze. Misha hoped that the hot weather would force the black lion to the waterhole. She knew lots of animals would gather there for water, especially on a sunny day like today. They were lucky that the hot weather hadn't dried up the waterhole yet.

The tourist truck was dark green with open sides. Ziggy **WHOOPED** with excitement when he saw it.

He had always wanted to go in one of these. There were a few tourists already in the vehicle. They had cameras around their necks and smiled and waved at Misha, Ziggy and Hanna.

Hanna greeted the driver, who had a salt-and-pepper beard and cornrows, then led Misha and Ziggy to their seats.

'Keep your hands inside the vehicle,' Hanna warned. 'We might pass some animals on the way to the waterhole. They may look cute and harmless, which would make you want to touch them. But, remember, they are wild and could be dangerous.'

The roads were **BUMPY** and the lady sitting in front of them winced every time they went over a **hump**, but Misha and Ziggy **loved it**. They were so different to the smooth and boring roads

in London. The twins **WHOOPED** every time they bounced in the air, until some of the other tourists glared at them and Hanna told them to quieten down, not without a smile on her face though.

'Here we are,' the driver eventually said. He stopped in the middle of the jungle and pointed to the grasslands. The greenery seemed to stretch on for miles and miles, and in the far distance were the highlands.

From her seat, Misha could see some warthogs already by the waterhole. All she needed to do was talk to them to find out about the black lion. They exited the tourist truck. The sun here was much stronger than anything the twins had ever experienced in London. Ziggy wished he could transform into a wild boar. They had the best way to cool off. They would roll themselves in mud, and when the mud evaporated, it also took away excess body heat. Instead, Ziggy and Misha felt like they were standing in the middle of an oven. Hanna fanned herself with her hand and held her cold water bottle to her neck.

The driver put on a straw hat. 'I'm Hawi, and I'll be your guide. Please follow me and stay as quiet as possible. We are here to observe, not to disturb the animals. *This is their home and we must respect it at all times.'*

They followed Hawi through the jungle and the dry grass scratched Misha's ankles. The warthogs heard their footsteps and ran away. Misha sighed, disappointed. A group of monkeys with beige-and-brown fur swung across the branches and landed by the waterhole. Hawi gestured for the tourists to move closer, but they stopped when one of the monkeys turned towards them. It had a red triangle on its throat and chest.

'That is amazing,' Hawi said excitedly. 'This is the gelada monkey, also known as the bleeding-heart monkey, and they are usually found in the highlands or the Simien Mountains National Park. It's very rare for them to come down here.'

The tourists immediately started taking pictures. There were four gelada monkeys. One was plucking up the grass and eating it, and the others were drinking from the waterhole. There were no signs of any lions at all, let alone the black lion.

'I need to talk to them,' Misha hissed to Ziggy. 'They might know something.'

'But how?' Ziggy whispered back. They needed a distraction. He looked around the grassy floor to try and find something and he almost fell over when he noticed the huge footprint on the ground. 'No way.' Ziggy put his own foot into it, and his foot was tiny compared to the print on the ground.

'Hawi?' Ziggy called. 'I think I found an **elephant's footprint!'**

CHAPTER SIX
Bribing a Gelada Monkey

The group gasped and hurried over. Ziggy nodded at Misha, who took a step back as everyone else rushed passed her. She knew she didn't have long before Hanna would notice she was gone, but she only needed a little bit of time. As everyone crowded around the elephant's footprint, Misha ran over to the monkeys, who stood alert when they saw her.

'Hello.' Misha waved and the monkeys looked at

each other, surprised. 'I'm Misha.'

The largest gelada monkey took a step forward and looked at Misha. 'How come we can understand you?' he questioned.

'I can speak to animals. It's a gift I have,' Misha explained. **'I promise, I mean no harm.'**

'Come, Kaleb,' a female monkey said from a distance. There was a young monkey standing slightly behind her that Misha hadn't noticed. 'We don't speak to humans. They're nothing but trouble.'

'I'm not. I would never hurt an animal,' Misha said. 'In fact, there's one I'm looking for and I heard he may be in danger.'

The other gelada monkeys turned their back on Misha, but Kaleb continued to stare. Misha didn't turn away and she prayed he would see that she was telling the truth.

'What animal?' Kaleb asked.

'The black lion.'

At the mention of the black lion, all of the gelada monkeys glared at Misha. The female one who had spoken out against humans **bared her teeth** and **JUMPED FORWARD** at Misha, as if to scare her, but Misha stood her ground.

'Stop it, Lelo!' Kaleb snapped. *'Can't you see that she's not like the rest? We can understand each other.'*

'What are you?' Lelo glared at Misha.

'I'm just a human, but a good one. Please. If the black lion is in danger, then I can help.'

'We're all in danger,' Lelo said. **'Because of humans who won't leave us alone.**

Now, please let us be. Come on, everyone.'

Misha's heart sank as the gelada monkeys started to walk away. The young one kept looking back at her. Kaleb waved at Misha regretfully.

How am I going to help Dad now? Misha put her head down and blinked quickly, trying not to let any tears fall, but then she felt a small furry hand in hers. Misha looked up and the young gelada monkey was beside her.

'I'm Negash.' He sniffed the air. 'Something smells good.'

Misha had almost forgotten about the wrapped-up fatira that she had put in her waist bag earlier. The other gelada monkeys were already at a distance and she didn't want Negash to get in trouble, but she had an idea.

'I have food. Do you want to try some?' Misha asked, and Negash nodded eagerly.

Misha took the fatira out of her bag and when Negash went for it, she quickly held it back. 'Only if you can tell me where the black lion is.'

Negash raised his eyebrows. 'I don't know why you want to see Jember. He is so grumpy and has no friends.'

'Why is that?' Misha asked, bending down so she was at eye level with the young monkey.

Negash shrugged his shoulders. 'Mama says **he hasn't got a pride**. But I think it's the **men that keep coming that are annoying him.**'

'The men?' Misha frowned. 'Can you tell me more?'

'That's all I know.' Negash looked at the fatira greedily. 'Can I have it now?'

'We had a deal, remember? Where's Jember?'

Negash pointed to the right, towards some thick bushes. 'Over there.' And when Misha turned to look, Negash **SNATCHED** her fatira out of her hand and ran in the direction of his family.

Misha was so busy thinking about how she was going to sneak into the bushes to find the black lion that she didn't hear the rest of the group coming towards her. She jumped when a strong hand fell on her shoulder.

'Hanna, you scared me!'

'What are you doing here?' Hanna put her hands on her hips. 'You're meant to stay with the group, not go wandering. It's not safe.'

'I'm sorry,' Misha said. She dipped her head and enlarged her eyes, the way she always did with adults if she ever got in trouble. They usually couldn't stay mad at her for long, and Hanna was no different.

'It's fine,' Hanna said, before she smiled. 'Ziggy found an elephant's footprint! And we learned some interesting facts – right, Zig?'

'Yep! A baby elephant is **massive!** It can weigh almost **ninety-one kilograms** and its *tusks* are actually **TEETH.**'

'That's very cool,' Misha said. 'I wonder if it's in the bushes.' She nodded her head towards the thick bush Negash had mentioned a few moments earlier, but Ziggy frowned at her.

Hanna laughed. 'I think we would see if an elephant was in the bush.'

'Maybe,' Misha said. 'Or something else could be in there.'

Ziggy continued to frown and Misha stared at him with a determined expression. She mouthed '*lion*' and Ziggy's eyes widened.

'Wait, I think I saw something,' he said quickly, pointing across the waterhole, and when Hanna turned to look, he placed his water bottle at the back of his shorts out of sight. 'Sorry, it must've been the sun playing tricks on me. Hanna, I think I left my bottle in the truck.'

'Oh no!' Hanna looked down at her own bottle,

which was almost empty. 'I would offer you mine, but I've nearly finished my water. I'll go back and get it for you. Stay right here, okay?'

'Okay,' the twins chorused.

'JINX!' Ziggy said, and Misha rolled her eyes.

'Not now, Zig.'

Hawi was busy talking to some of the tourists, and the others were posing for pictures. No one was paying any attention to them.

'Come on,' Misha said, grabbing Ziggy's arm and leading him towards the bulky bushes.

CHAPTER SEVEN
Jember

The bushes were large and lush, a bright green that seemed to glisten in the sun. Vibrant red-and-yellow flowers blossomed in the grass.

Misha's heart was racing. She couldn't believe she was going to come face to face with a lion. She prayed that she could get her words out to help him before he decided that she would be the perfect meal!

Ziggy's heart was pounding too. He couldn't believe that he would be able to shapeshift into a lion. Maybe if the black lion didn't want to meet Dad, Ziggy could go in his place. Anything to make sure Dad's documentary was a success.

And Misha and Ziggy were both nervous because they had broken Dad's rules, so they knew they would be in a *lot* of trouble.

A low **growl** came from behind the bush and Misha and Ziggy looked at each other.

'Hello?' Misha said. 'Is that Jember?'

But there was no response.

'Pull the bush back,' Ziggy encouraged.

'No, you pull it back!' Misha argued.

The truth was, both of them were scared.

'Together?' Ziggy asked, and Misha nodded.

'One, two, three . . .'

They pulled back the bush and large amber eyes stared back at them. Misha and Ziggy marvelled at the lion's mane, which started off as golden brown and then glistened into deep chocolate brown and then jet black. It travelled past his shoulders, all the way down to his belly. **He was the most beautiful creature they had ever seen.**

'Jember?' Misha asked.

Jember took a step forward and the twins instinctively took a step back. But when Jember took another step, Ziggy noticed that his left back leg was slightly buckled.

'He's hurt,' Ziggy said, as he pointed to Jember's slightly raised back paw.

'OH NO!' Misha gasped, wondering what had

happened to him. 'I'm Misha. We've been looking for you. Are you hurt?'

Jember's eyes never left Misha. Even though Misha wanted to turn away from his strong stare, she kept eye contact, knowing that was one way for animals to trust her.

'How is this possible?' Jember asked in a low growl. 'We can understand each other?'

'I can speak to animals. It's a gift that I have,' Misha explained. 'This is my twin brother, Ziggy.

He has a gift too. He can shapeshift into any animal he's physically close to. That means he can turn into you. Do you want to see?'

Jember's attention turned to Ziggy, who was practically jumping on the spot waiting for a chance to shapeshift. Slowly Jember nodded. Ziggy closed his eyes and his skin turned **furry and thick**, his spine **elongated** and he fell forward onto **four legs**. Jember's eyes widened when Ziggy stood in front of him, a reflection of himself.

'THIS IS SO COOL!' Ziggy shouted, and Misha shushed him. To anyone else, though, it would have sounded like a **ROAR**.

Ziggy couldn't believe he was a **real-life lion!** Finally, he was an animal that was super cool and so different to what he was used to transforming into. He wanted to **RUN** and **HUNT** and **SWIM** and **JUMP** and **CLIMB** in his new body, but he knew it wouldn't be the best idea. Maybe later he could find time to really see what life was like as a lion. Jember seemed to be more comfortable around another lion because, after a short moment, he lay down on the ground and his eyes softened.

'How did you get hurt?' Misha asked softly.

'Poachers tried to steal me,' he said.

'POACHERS?' Misha and Ziggy said at the same time. Usually one of them would shout 'jinx', but they knew that poachers were a very serious issue, so this didn't feel like the right time for games.

Dad had told them all about poachers. They are terrible people who hunt animals for their fur, their skin, their teeth, their claws and many other parts of their bodies to sell them for money or keep as a prize or ornament that they can hang in their houses. **Poachers don't care about the lives of animals.** Black lions were rare because of their unique black mane, and that made them even more of a target for poachers to capture.

'I saw their snare and avoided it,' Jember said, 'but one of them threw something hard at my leg to try and slow me down. I managed to escape them, but they'll be back. **Those men don't give up easily.**'

Misha wanted to tell her dad. He would know what to do, but she didn't want to frighten Jember with even more humans. And how would she explain to Dad that she had somehow found the black lion? That would mean admitting to him that she and Ziggy had broken his rules, and it would also mean revealing the truth about their powers, which they had been told never to do.

Ziggy's ears turned from side to side. He could hear footsteps from at least a mile away.

'Warthogs,' Jember said, and instantly Ziggy's mouth watered.

Mmmm. He would love to try a big, fat, juicy warthog. Ziggy shook his head in disgust. That was the lion side of him. Definitely not his **REAL HUMAN SIDE!**

'Okay, I have an idea, Jember,' Misha said, interrupting her brother's thoughts. 'We're staying in a treehouse not far from here. Tonight, I will shine a torch from the top of our house so you

know that it's us. Then you can follow the light from the torch to find us. We'll meet you at the front of our house. We can see that you prefer being around another black lion, so Ziggy will shapeshift into one to make you feel comfortable. Our dad is a wildlife TV presenter and his film crew always carry first-aid kits for the animals they film, just in case they are hurt or need help. We'll bring a first-aid kit with us and we can mend your back leg. How does that sound?'

Jember narrowed his eyes. *'You would do that for me? And there's no catch?'*

Misha wanted to mention Dad's documentary and that they had flown here all the way from England to film him, but she knew that would only scare Jember off. Helping him with his injury was far more important.

'No catch,' Misha said. 'Right, Zig?'

But Ziggy was too busy thinking about all of the cool things he wanted to try in his new lion form.

CHAPTER EIGHT
An Ambitious Plan

As Misha and Ziggy walked back towards the group, they saw Hanna looking around in a panic. When she saw them, her forehead crinkled into a deep frown. Misha and Ziggy gulped. They knew they were in big trouble.

'I told you both not to sneak off! **WE HEARD A LION ROAR.** Hawi said it was probably miles away, as a lion's roar can travel.' Hanna shuddered.

Ziggy smiled smugly, taking pride that it was him.

'We're sorry, Hanna,' Misha said quickly. 'We got excited seeing all the animals and followed a monkey through the bush. Right, Zig?'

'Yes, sorry!' Ziggy said. 'But we got you these.' He presented Hanna with a small handful of flowers.

Ziggy had had the bright idea to pick the pretty red-and-yellow flowers they'd seen in the bush.

The flowers brought a smile to Hanna's face, but only for a moment. 'Thank you for these, but your dad was very clear about the rules. You're not allowed to be alone around wild animals, so now you won't leave my sight!'

Misha, Ziggy and Hanna rejoined the rest of the tourists at the waterhole. They saw hyenas, antelopes

and zebras, but there was no sign of the elephant who had left the footprint.

When the waterhole tour was finished, they decided to visit Mercato Market.

Mercato Market was the largest open-air market in all of Africa. There were so many stalls and people selling everything from clothes, to food, to electronics, to jewellery.

The market was busy and **loud** and **colourful**. Any other day, Misha would have had the best time, but now all she wanted to do was get back to the treehouse and figure out how they could get Dad to film Jember without Jember getting angry and running away. If Dad left without any footage, he would be so sad. Then he would have to come back to Ethiopia, and she and Ziggy

would be apart from him for weeks again.

Misha looked over at Ziggy, who didn't seem to have a care in the world. She could always ask him to transform so that Dad could film him as if he was the real black lion, but the idea of lying to Dad made her stomach tighten into knots.

Misha and Ziggy arrived back at the treehouse by the evening, exhausted from their day out. Their dad stood up when they walked in.

'Hey, guys! How was your day?'

'So much fun!' Misha skipped over to him, and her dad gave her a tight hug, before he reached out and pulled Ziggy in.

'We saw gelada monkeys, an elephant footprint,

warthogs, hyenas, antelopes and zebras,' Ziggy said excitedly as he eased himself out of the hug he shared with Misha and Dad.

'Gelada monkeys?' Dad's eyes widened. 'Wow, that's a rare sight in these parts of the country.'

'Did you find the black lion?' Misha and Ziggy asked in unison, and Ziggy quickly shouted **'JINX!'** before Misha could.

Their dad smiled at them, but then said sadly, 'No, we didn't. But we did manage to get some footage of some other wild animals, which is super exciting. Hopefully, it won't be long until we see the black lion.'

'You definitely will!' Ziggy said, and Misha glared at him. Ziggy shouldn't promise that Dad would see Jember – he was still frightened of other humans. 'I mean, I hope you will.'

'Thanks, Zig.' Dad ruffled Ziggy's hair.

After they spoke more about their day, Dad went to talk to the crew, and Ziggy noticed a bag full of supplies. Ziggy pocketed a pair of binoculars and a torch and grabbed the first-aid kit – they would need that for later!

The adults were in deep discussion, so Ziggy pointed upstairs and Misha nodded. The views from the top floor were incredible. The stars were twinkling and the moon looked like it was hovering just over the waterhole.

92

The animals seemed to be out. Misha could hear them arguing about **where to sleep tonight** and talking about WHERE TO HUNT TOMORROW, their voices blending into one another. She wished she was with them and could join in the conversation.

'I want to live here,' Ziggy said. 'I feel at home.'

'Me too,' Misha said. 'After dinner, we'll use the torch to signal to Jember and then you'll have to sneak out to bandage him up.'

'Me?' Ziggy asked, surprised. Misha was the responsible one.

'I can't sneak out with all these adults awake, can I? But you can shapeshift into the black lion, put Jember's mind at ease, and then transform back into your human form to help him.'

At that moment, Ziggy wished that Misha had

his power too. *What if I can't help Jember? What if something goes wrong?* he thought to himself. He felt Misha's soft hand in his.

'You've got this,' she said confidently.

Ziggy sighed. He didn't feel like it, but if Misha believed in him, then maybe **he should believe in himself too.**

CHAPTER NINE
Two Heads Are Better Than One

One of the great things about Misha and Ziggy's amazing treehouse was that they could cook outside on the barbecue. Everyone chipped in with preparing the meal. The twins were in charge of drinks and had to carry multiple jugs outside to the fold-out table lit up with candles.

The table was soon packed with all different sorts of food. But even though Misha was hungry, she felt too anxious to eat. Ziggy's plate, however, was stuffed high and his mouth was covered in barbecue sauce.

'MMMM, SO GOOD!' he said for what felt like the millionth time.

Dad laughed, before shooting a concerned look at Misha. 'Everything okay, Mish? Are you feeling well? You need to eat something.'

Misha nodded and picked up a chicken wing. The last thing she needed was Dad keeping an extra eye on her tonight.

'It's so beautiful.' Hanna sighed. 'I could stay out here all night.'

All the adults agreed, and Ziggy mouthed, '*Do something!*' to Misha. How were they going to help Jember if the adults wouldn't go inside the house?

'Oh, you know what would be cool?' Misha said quickly. 'A game! What's that one you like again, Dad?'

Dad frowned. 'Charades?'

'That's the one! Let's play a round . . . but inside, because the lighting is better.'

Dad rubbed his hands together. He was very competitive when it came to games, and Misha knew he wouldn't be able to resist.

'I'll bring in the plates,' Ziggy said, standing to his feet, grabbing the plates and taking them inside.

'Oh, thanks, Zig,' Dad said.

'I'll get you a binbag,' Misha offered, following closely behind.

After putting the plates in the kitchen, Ziggy waited by the door and discreetly handed Misha

the binoculars and torch he had found earlier, then headed back outside to the rest of the group. Misha held them close to her chest as she walked quickly into the house. Once she closed the door, Misha ran, two steps at a time, up the stairs and to the window on the very top floor. The binoculars weren't very helpful because it was so dark outside, so she turned on the torch and its **bright light** stretched out over the trees.

'Come on, Jember,' Misha whispered.

Misha couldn't have the torch on too long in

case someone downstairs saw its bright light. She could only hope that Jember would see it before she turned it off.

Ziggy made his way back to the house carrying more dirty plates when he saw the light from Misha's torch disappear. Luckily, Dad and the others had been too busy chatting away to notice.

'Binbag,' Misha said as Ziggy opened the door.

'Thanks,' Ziggy said.

She handed it to him, and he could feel something inside it. Misha gave him a knowing look.

'Come on, Dad,' Misha said, interrupting the adults' conversation. 'Let's show them how we play charades.'

'You've got it!' Dad said as Misha led him inside the house.

The door was left ajar for Ziggy and as soon as they were out of earshot, Ziggy ran outside, turned the binbag upside down, and the first-aid kit and torch fell out. Ziggy turned the torch on and waved it in front of him, but there was no sign of Jember. Ziggy knew his hearing was a **MILLION TIMES BETTER** as a lion than in human form, so with one quick look back at the house, Ziggy transformed into a black lion.

Maybe Jember needs some help finding us? Ziggy thought. So he decided to meet him by the trees closest to the house.

Ziggy waited. His ears kept turning from left to right as he picked up sounds from all over. Suddenly he could hear quick footsteps. *Jember?* Ziggy let out a low **GROWL**. Not loud enough to draw the attention of his family, but loud enough for Jember to hear, who sounded like he was nearby. A twig creaked from somewhere close and then the footsteps suddenly stopped. Ziggy's heart started to race, but he wasn't sure why. Suddenly he could hear more than one set of footsteps. Ziggy **GROWLED AGAIN**, not caring who heard this time, but there still was no sign of Jember. Before he knew it, Ziggy felt something tight, uncomfortable and painful around his neck. He tried to wiggle, but whatever it was felt even tighter.

'Now we've got you,' a deep voice hissed in the darkness.

CHAPTER TEN
Where is Ziggy?

ad was **FLAPPING HIS ARMS** and **jutting out his neck**, making everyone laugh. Misha was just about to shout out what she thought he was, when she suddenly felt **cold** all over, almost like someone had tipped an ice bucket over her body. She didn't know how, and maybe it was just a twin thing, but she knew something bad had happened to Ziggy.

Misha abruptly stood up, hugging herself despite

the heat as she was now freezing cold.

'Everything okay, Mish?' Dad asked, mid flap.

'I'm fine.' She forced a smile. 'I'll just help Ziggy so he can join in.'

Misha didn't wait for Dad to respond. She hurried to the front door and gently closed it behind her as she stepped outside.

'Ziggy?' she hissed, but there was no answer. She made her way to the trees closest to the house, but Ziggy was nowhere to be seen. Instead, the torch and first-aid kit were lying on the ground.

Where was he?

From the shadows, a pair of amber eyes stared at her.

'Ziggy?' Misha said again, hurrying towards him, but as she got closer, the black lion stepped forward.

'It's me, Jember,' the black lion said in his low, deep voice.

Misha's heart started to race. 'If you're here, where's Ziggy?'

'The men that I told you about. The poachers. They were in the bush. I tried to avoid them as I made my way to meet Ziggy, but Ziggy had shapeshifted into a black lion and the **poachers caught him.**'

'What?' Misha was terrified. Ziggy was gone, taken by very bad men. *What if they hurt him? How do I tell Dad?* **WE HAVE TO FIND ZIGGY. WE HAVE TO RESCUE HIM!** Misha cried.

'It's okay,' Jember said. He rubbed the side of his face against her arm, which reminded her of her cat, Fergie, and she instantly calmed down.

Misha ran her hand over Jember's head, and he **purred**. 'I know where they are, but we have to be quick.'

'Is your foot okay? Can you manage the journey?' Misha asked, thinking of the first-aid kit still on the ground.

'It will be fine. Let's go and rescue Ziggy.'

Misha took one last look at the house, knowing that in a few minutes, Dad would be outside wondering why she and Ziggy were taking so long. He would be worried sick when he realized that they'd vanished. But Misha had to find Ziggy. She didn't feel whole without him.

'Okay,' Misha said. She looked up to the twinkly stars and whispered, **'ZIGGY, I'M COMING.'** She hoped he could hear her, wherever he was.

Meanwhile, on the other side of the waterhole, Ziggy was being dragged through the bushes. There was one man holding on to him and two more in front. They all looked the same in the dim light. Tall with white skin, wearing khaki long-sleeved tops with matching combat pants, and black boots. They looked like they were going to war, and they each carried weapons. Ziggy tried to scare them with **his roar and his big, sharp teeth**, but all they did was pull on whatever it was around his neck, which hurt a lot and made him fall quiet. All he could hope was that Misha would be able to find him, and quick.

The poachers' campsite was much less fancy than Misha and Ziggy's treehouse. There were dirty plates and pans on the ground, broken camp furniture lying around and a huge tent that was torn all over. But what made Ziggy's heart go still was the metal cage with steel bars standing in front of him.

'Welcome to your new home,' one of the men said, and Ziggy gulped.

They forced him into the cage and the metal floor was cold under his paws. The men began to celebrate, toasting each other on a great victory. The cage was barely big enough for him to turn around in. He had no idea what they were going to do with him, but he remembered all the information Dad had told him and Misha about poachers, and he knew that poachers usually killed the animals they caught. Or they would sell them, which was just as bad because that meant that he would be LOST FOREVER.

Ziggy peered through the steel bars and looked at the grass, hoping to see a snake so he could shapeshift into one and slither away to escape, but there weren't any animals around. His mind was racing so much, he couldn't even think of any small animals he had shapeshifted into before that he could try to transform into now. Plus, what if the poachers saw him use his power?

What if I never see Misha, Dad, Grandma Yinka, Grandma Joy and Grandpa Tunde again? What about my friends at school? And Blue and Fergie? What if the last people I see are these horrible men?

A tear fell down Ziggy's furry face. He looked up into the starry sky and whispered, 'Misha, where are you?' He wished she would rescue him soon.

CHAPTER ELEVEN
Animals Riot

Misha and Jember were hidden behind a tall tree, but they could see the poachers' campsite. In the far corner was a caged Ziggy. Misha wanted to run up to him, to let him know that she was here to rescue him, but she had to tread carefully. She wondered why he hadn't transformed and escaped, but then she saw the weapons and she gasped. He must be so scared. She knew that she was, and if she wasn't quick, the poachers were going to do something terrible to her brother.

'We need a distraction,' Jember said. 'These men aren't afraid of anything and don't care about hurting animals, so whatever it is, it needs to be something that will take them by surprise.'

'Like what?' Misha said. Her mind was unusually blank.

Above them, Misha saw an animal swing across the branches. The birds were conversing in their nests in the trees, and Misha smiled slowly. 'I know what to do. Follow me.'

They retraced their steps, heading back further into the bushes. Misha held her torch up to the trees and a **black bird** with a **scattering of white feathers** and a **LONG BEAK** peered down at her.

'That's a wattled ibis,' Jember said. 'And they can get pretty **loud.**'

Misha recognized the birds from the research she and Ziggy had done before they left for Ethiopia. And loud was exactly what Misha was counting on.

'Hello,' Misha said, and the wattled ibis peered curiously at her. 'My name is Misha, and I really need your help. *Poachers have captured my brother.*'

'Poachers?' the wattled ibis said.

'Who said *poachers*?' another voice said.

'They're back again?' a third voice spoke.

Misha swept her torch across the tree and saw there were at least fifty of the birds.

'I want to get rid of the poachers once and for all, but I need your help, and with as many animals as possible. *Will you help me?*'

'Of course!' The wattled ibis flew down and landed next to Misha. '*I hate them!*' It jumped when it saw Jember.

'He's okay. He won't hurt you,' Misha said quickly. 'What's your name?'

'Aisha, and I have lots of brothers –' Aisha pointed back at the trees above them and rolled her eyes – 'as you can see. They are annoying, but if any of them were in trouble, I would help them too.'

'Thank you,' Misha said gratefully. 'We'll have to be quick though.'

'Oh, don't worry. We've got these.' Aisha waved her wings. 'I'll go and find Selam – she owes me a favour too. Elephants are always asking for something or other.'

'An elephant!' Misha gasped. 'That would be brilliant.'

'Leave it with me, Misha,' Aisha said. 'We'll meet you back here.' Aisha let out a loud *haa-haa-haa-haa* call that fifty of her siblings responded back to.

If that didn't **WAKE UP** the jungle, Misha didn't know what would!

Ziggy lay down on his paws and sighed deeply. By now he had learned the names of the poachers. There was Ian with the beard, who Ziggy assumed was the leader, as the others always asked him questions. Mac with the tattoos on his arm. And Harry with the glasses, who kept popping pieces of chewing gum in his mouth and Ziggy saw it every time he spoke.

Haa-haa-haa-haa.

Ziggy lifted his head when he heard the loud bird call. It was so loud that it made the poachers stop talking.

'what is that racket?' Ian asked, and the rest shrugged.

'Maybe we should check it out?' Harry suggested.

'What about that one?' Mac asked, jerking his thumb at Ziggy, and they all looked at him.

Ziggy hoped that they would leave so that maybe he could shapeshift into anything he could remember and escape.

Ian opened up another drink and slurped it down

noisily. 'It's just birds. Let's get an early night and deal with this one in the morning.'

Ziggy had no idea what 'deal with this one' meant. *Are they going to hurt me? Ship me off somewhere?* All he knew was that he wasn't going to see his family ever again. He slumped back onto his paws, trying his best not to cry.

Ian, Mac and Harry sat in their fold-out chairs. Mac and Harry were snoring loudly, but Ian was still wide awake. His chair was angled towards Ziggy and his weapon was by his feet. Ian stood up and walked close to Ziggy's cage. Ziggy stood on his four legs and glared at him.

'You're going to look so pretty in someone's living room,' Ian said, with a menacing grin.

'GO AWAY!' Ziggy said, but it came out as a loud

roar that made Ian stumble back and Mac and Harry jump up awake.

'I'll let this beast know who's boss!' Ian snarled as Harry and Mac smirked.

Ziggy closed his eyes and squeezed them tight. *This is it*, he thought. *This is the end. I love you Misha, Dad, Grandma Yinka, Grandma Joy, Grandpa Tunde, Fergie, Blue—*

A loud **TRUMPET SOUND** came from somewhere not too far away. Ziggy slowly opened his eyes and Ian, Mac and Harry ran to the edge of the campsite.

'Is that an elephant?' Harry asked slowly.

Ziggy remembered the elephant's footprint on the ground by the waterhole!

The trumpet came again, but this time it was accompanied by a loud **roar** and the *haa-haa-haa-*

haa call of the birds. Ziggy squinted his eyes at what looked like a black cloud coming towards them. Suddenly the trees parted and an elephant walked through the clearing. Surrounding its feet were various animals – **wolves**, *monkeys*, **hyenas**, **ORYX** – and right at the front was **Jember**, with **MISHA BESIDE HIM.**

'You came!' Ziggy roared, and Misha waved at him. He was so relieved to see his twin sister.

'Quick, grab everything!' Ian said. He picked up his rucksack and weapon. 'We need to go.'

'But what about the lion?' Mac asked.

Harry pointed a trembling finger up to the sky as he stepped back. 'I . . . hate . . .'

'Birds.' Ziggy grinned.

The black birds with white feathers swarmed into

the campsite in a circle. The poachers ducked and covered their heads as the birds **PECKED** at them from above and flapped their wings in the poachers' faces. Ziggy watched the chaos in amusement. The monkeys ran in and grabbed the dirty pots and pans and began to **bang** them. The wolves **DESTROYED** all the camp furniture, and the oryx dragged the sleeping bags out of the tent and **RIPPED** them to pieces. The hyenas **stole** whatever food they could find, making sure they fed their hungry stomachs and left the poachers with nothing.

'Oh, Ziggy!' Misha ran to him and held her hands on to the bars. 'Did they hurt you?'

'I'm okay,' Ziggy said. 'How did you find me?'

'It was Jember. He saw the poachers capture you and knew where they would be keeping you. And

all the animals were happy to help us rescue you. But, why didn't you transform?'

'I wanted to, but I was just so scared, my brain couldn't think of any animals. And I couldn't risk the poachers seeing me shapeshift!'

Misha reached through the bars and ran her hand through his thick fur. 'Don't worry, I'll get you out of there.' She turned to the animals and cupped her hands on either side of her mouth. **'EVERYONE, STOP!'** she shouted.

Instantly it went quiet and they all looked at Misha. The poachers whimpered on the floor. Jember was hovering over them and **growling**.

'Who's in charge here?' Misha asked the poachers.

Mac and Harry pointed at Ian, who looked like he was going to cry.

Misha put her hands on her hips. 'How dare you come here and steal these animals. They don't belong to you and they have had enough of you and your poacher friends coming into their homes and ruining where they live and destroying their lives. Open this cage right now. And take this thing off from around his neck.'

Ian's hands shook as he pulled the keys out of his pocket. Jember **roared again**, this time more **FEROCIOUSLY**, and Ian screamed. He scrambled to his feet, ran to the cage and unlocked it, sobbing as he removed the cord from around Ziggy's neck.

Ziggy made his way out of the cage, taking long strides and stretching his neck now that he was free. Misha threw herself at him, wrapping her arms around his furry body.

127

'Thanks, sis. I knew you'd come to rescue me,' Ziggy said with the brightest smile on his face. 'What are we going to do with *them*?' He looked over to Ian, Mac and Harry. They were all huddled against a tree, shielding themselves from the animals.

Misha smiled. 'That's Selam over there –' she pointed at the elephant, who was patiently waiting by the campsite – 'and she's going to handle it.'

'Dawit, give the poachers' weapons to Selam, please,' Misha instructed, and one of the wolves grabbed the dangerous items with its mouth and placed them at Selam's feet. Selam stepped on them and they broke in half. She looked at Misha, who gave her the **thumbs-up**.

With one swoop of her trunk, Selam made the poachers' tent collapse to the floor. Then she rolled the fabric around the poachers. They looked like a filling inside a burrito. They tried to squirm and move their bodies, but they were **STUCK!** Selam then lifted and held them in her trunk, wrapped up in the tent, and slowly began to make her way back into the bushes. The poachers' **SCREAMS** echoed throughout the jungle.

'Where is she taking them?' Ziggy asked.

'To the police station. **Poaching is illegal**, so they're going to be in **big trouble**.' Misha laughed.

She thanked all the animals and they began to make their way home until it was just Misha, Ziggy and Jember left.

'Thank you again, Jember,' Misha said. She scratched him behind his ears and he **purred**.

Ziggy's ears moved quickly back and forth. He could hear rapid footsteps. *Oh no! Are there more poachers approaching?*

'Misha!' a familiar voice called from nearby. 'Ziggy!'

'Dad!' Misha said. 'Quick, Zig, transform.'

But Ziggy shook his head. 'I want Dad to get his footage of the black lion. Once he does, I'll hurry

131

back to the house before he gets there. Jember, thank you for helping to save my life, but I think you should go before they arrive. Our dad won't hurt you, but it's better to be safe than sorry.'

To their surprise, Jember didn't move. '**Because of you, the poachers are finally gone. And me and all the other animals here are safe.** If your dad is as brilliant as you two, then I want to meet him. Besides, what's better than one black lion? Two!'

Misha and Ziggy looked at each other in shock. But it was nothing compared to the surprise on the faces of their dad and Ed, who stumbled through the bushes with torches and came to a standstill when they saw Misha standing in between **TWO BLACK LIONS!**

CHAPTER TWELVE
Not One, But Two Black Lions

'Misha,' Dad whispered, eyeing the lions beside her. He held his hands out to her. 'I want you to walk over to me slowly. Ed, we need a distraction.'

'Dad, it's okay,' Misha said. **'THEY'RE FRIENDLY.'**

'Friendly!' Dad exclaimed. He had a point. Lions weren't known for their friendliness.

Misha knew that Grandma Yinka had told them to keep their powers a secret, but Dad was wasting

133

time worrying about her being in danger rather than filming the TWO black lions! Misha put one hand each on top of Jember's and Ziggy's heads and they both nuzzled against her. Dad's and Ed's mouths dropped open.

Misha laughed. 'I told you! Quick, Dad, get them on camera before they leave.'

'Oh, yes, of course.' Dad tried to smooth down his T-shirt, which was ruffled from all the running he'd just done to find Misha and Ziggy. 'Wait, we left the camera at the house!'

'I can use this.' Ed pulled out his phone. 'It should be okay.'

Misha ran to Ed's side so she was out of view as her dad stepped in front of the camera. Misha pointed at her eyes and Dad quickly adjusted his glasses.

He smiled broadly and said, 'Now, you can see behind me what I've found. The reason why we've come all the way to Ethiopia . . .'

And Dad was in the zone, now transformed into the award-winning wildlife TV presenter Dayo Asotun as he began to share all the amazing and interesting facts about black lions. Jember lay down on all fours, looking slightly bored, but Ziggy seemed rooted to the spot, almost as if he had **STAGE FRIGHT!**

'Relax,' Misha whispered to him. Ed glanced at her, and she smiled innocently.

Ziggy glanced at Jember and copied his stance. When Jember put his head down, so did Ziggy. When Jember yawned, Ziggy yawned. Misha had to stop herself from laughing. Dad was too busy

talking into the camera to pay attention.

Suddenly Jember stood up and walked towards Dad. Ed gasped and Dad's eyes widened as he turned around. Ziggy copied suit and Dad took a step back as the two lions approached him at the same time. Jember brushed against Dad's chest before he winked at Misha and headed towards the bushes. Ziggy did the same, but he was a bit too forceful, and Dad almost fell over! Ed filmed them until they disappeared, and Misha knew that Ziggy would be heading back to the treehouse.

'Did you get that?' Dad exclaimed, and Ed nodded.

Dad picked Misha up and swung her around, cheering at the top of his voice. **'THAT WAS INCREDIBLE!** Everyone's going to be so happy!'

'Well done, Dad!' Misha beamed, even though it was really she and Ziggy who had done all the hard work. Speaking of Ziggy, she thought it best to remind Dad that he still hadn't found him. 'We still don't know where Ziggy is, do we?'

'OH NO, ZIGGY! I got so caught up with the lions.' Dad looked from left to right, as if Ziggy would appear from out of thin air. 'Where could he be? It's so dangerous out here, especially at this time of night.'

'I think we should check back at the house. You know Ziggy. He probably wandered off by accident and now he'll be hungry.'

'He must be so scared,' Dad said with worry. 'Let's hurry back.'

Dad held on to Misha's hand. As they walked through the bush and back towards the treehouse,

Misha tried very hard to not say hello to all the animals that greeted and thanked her for getting rid of those pesky poachers.

'Wow, they're really loud tonight, aren't they?' Dad said, and Misha smiled to herself.

Jember walked Ziggy as close to the house as he could get. Hanna was on the veranda, hugging herself tight as she looked anxiously into the darkness.

'Thanks again, Jember, for saving my life and also helping my dad. You don't know how much that means to him.'

'It was my pleasure,' Jember said. **'If it wasn't for you and your sister, those horrible**

poachers would still be sniffing around. We owe you a great debt.'

Ziggy sighed. 'I guess I'd better head in.' Despite being captured, he'd loved being a lion and wished he could stay like this for longer, but if he wasn't back in his human form by the time Dad got home, he would be in even more trouble. Ziggy transformed, double checking his nose to make sure the whiskers weren't still there.

'Take care of yourself, Jember,' Ziggy said, hugging him. Jember's fur was so soft against his skin.

'You too, special one, and your sister,' Jember replied.

It didn't take long for Jember to blend in with the darkness. Ziggy took a deep breath and stepped

into the clearing. Hanna gasped when she saw him, ran out of the house and pulled him into a big, tight hug.

'Ziggy, we've been so worried! Are you okay?'

'*Mmmm* . . .' Ziggy tried to speak, but the hug was so tight, he could barely get any words out!

Misha, Dad and Ed appeared not too long after

with Lexi and Carter, who had also been out searching for the twins in an area nearby. Misha did a great job pretending she hadn't seen Ziggy since he went missing.

'Don't pull a stunt like that again,' she said. 'You had us all worried.'

'Sorry,' Ziggy said softly.

Dad bent down so he was at eye level with Ziggy and kissed his forehead. 'You gave us such a scare, Zig. Where did you go?'

Everyone looked at him. Ziggy hadn't thought of a story, so he figured he would tell the truth. Well, sort of. 'I saw the black lion and I followed him so I could tell you where he was. But I got lost.'

'Oh, Zig.' Dad pulled him in tight. 'I know you were trying to help, but that was very dangerous.'

142

'I'm sorry. I guess you still haven't got your footage then?'

Dad and Ed shared a look.

Lexi gasped. 'You found it?'

'Found *them*,' Dad explained. 'There were two black lions and **WE GOT THEM ON VIDEO!'**

CHAPTER THIRTEEN
That's a Wrap

The end credits rolled on the TV screen and everyone clapped and cheered. Misha, Ziggy and Dad were back in England, and Dad's Ethiopian travel TV documentary was gaining a positive reaction from everyone who'd watched it.

'THAT WAS SO GOOD, DAD!' Misha said.

Ziggy was still speechless that he was on TV!

Dad grinned. 'I'm so glad you like it. The network

couldn't believe how friendly the black lions were. I wish I'd shown them how close Misha was to them.'

Grandma Joy glared at him. 'My granddaughter should never have been anywhere near them!' she moaned for the hundredth time.

At least Grandpa Tunde thought it was cool, although he did say it quietly and when Grandma Joy was out of the room.

Misha and Ziggy had got to spend the rest of the Ethiopia trip exploring the beautiful country. They'd visited the Simien Mountains National Park, and it had been even more fun because Dad had been with them and they'd finally seen a **leopard!** Misha had even seen Negash and his family again, although his mother, Lelo, had still been cold towards her. They didn't see Jember

again, but Misha and Ziggy knew they had made a

FRIEND FOR LIFE, and maybe one day they would

see him if they returned to Ethiopia.

Grandma Joy and Grandpa Tunde were full of

tales from their Caribbean cruise, and even though

it hadn't been Dad's first choice for Misha and

Ziggy to come with him to Ethiopia, he admitted

that he was glad they had been there.

Who knew – maybe this would be the start of more family trips?

'What are the chances of you finding *two* black lions?' Grandpa Tunde said, still in disbelief. Misha and Ziggy grinned at each other.

'I know! I was so lucky,' Dad said.

Luck has nothing to do with it, Misha thought.

Grandma Joy changed the channel to the news.

'**I can't believe I get to be on TV!**' Ziggy whispered to Misha. He may not have been as natural as Jember, but maybe more trips with Dad would make him comfortable in front of the camera.

'. . . *And finally, three poachers who were searching for the rare black lion have been arrested in Ethiopia.*'

'It couldn't be,' Misha said under her breath, but

the pictures of Ian, Mac and Harry appeared on the screen.

'No way!' Ziggy said.

Grandpa Tunde pointed at the screen. 'That's what you were looking for!'

'And what we found – twice!' Dad responded gleefully.

'Ah, that could have been very dangerous, Dayo, especially with the children.' Grandma Joy tutted. She seemed to forget that Misha and Ziggy were only in Ethiopia because she and Grandpa Tunde were on holiday!

'Thank goodness we got footage of the black lions and they are now safe and sound. **They're magical creatures and deserve to survive in the wild,'** Dad said.

'You're right, Dad, they do,' Misha said. 'Come, Ziggy, I want to show you something.' Misha hooked on to Ziggy's arm and dragged him up the stairs to their bedroom. 'Can you believe it?'

'Because of your smart plan to rescue me, you also rescued *all* the other animals in the wild from those evil poachers!' Ziggy beamed.

'And not only did we find Jember, but because of you, Dad was able to film *two* black lions for his TV documentary,' Misha squealed.

Misha and Ziggy **FIST-BUMPED** each other.

'Seems like Dad needs us on these trips,' Ziggy said.

'Definitely.' Misha grinned.

And they both wondered what **GREAT ADVENTURE** would be waiting for them next.

FUN FACTS ABOUT BLACK LIONS

1. **What makes black lions different?**
    Black lions are different from normal lions because they have darker manes, are better hunters and are more dominant so can defend their pride better.

2. **What is another name for the black lion?**
    Another name for the black lion is the Abyssinian lion.

3. **Where do black lions live?**
    Black lions live in Ethiopia and the Kalahari Desert in South Africa.

4. **What do black lions eat?**
    Black lions are carnivores which means they have a meat-based diet. They mainly eat large mammals like zebras and antelopes, but if food is hard to find they will eat reptiles and even insects.

5. **What do black lions drink?**
    Black lions drink water.

6. **How long do black lions live?**
    A black lion can live up to fourteen years in the wild.

7.   What are a group of lions called?
A group of lions is called a pride.

8.   Who do black lions live with?
Black lions, like all lions, live in a pride. A lion pride is mainly made up of female lions and their cubs, with also two to four male lions.

9.   What size is a typical lion pride?
A lion pride can range from just two lions up to forty lions.

10.   Who are the main hunters — female or male lions?
The main hunters are female lions, also known as lionesses. They provide food for the pride.

11.   Who stays with the pride?
Lions (male) stay with the cubs in the pride to protect them, while the lionesses leave the pride to hunt.

12.   How far can a black lion's roar be heard?
A black lion's roar is the loudest of all of the big cats and can be heard up to five miles away.

13.   How do black lions mark their territory?

Black lions mark their territory by roaring to warn other lions to stay away. Black lions will also use their scent to mark their territory, including rubbing their bodies against grass, scraping their paws on the ground and urinating.

14. How long do black lions sleep?

Black lions can sleep for a long time – up to twenty-one hours.

15. Are black lions endangered and if so, why?

Black lions are endangered because of poaching, climate change and their natural habitat being destroyed for many reasons, including removing trees and bushes to build homes for humans.

INTERESTING FACTS
ABOUT ETHIOPIA

1. **Where is Ethiopia?**

    Ethiopia is in East Africa. It's Africa's second most populated nation.

2. **What countries are next to Ethiopia?**

    The countries that are next to Ethiopia are Kenya, Somalia, Sudan and Eritrea.

3. **Does Ethiopia have a different calendar and if so, why?**

    Ethiopia has a different calendar to the rest of the world. They are eight years behind us! This is because Ethiopia calculates the birth year of Jesus Christ differently to the western world.

4. **Can you name some popular Ethiopian food?**

    Some popular Ethiopian food is injera, tibs, daro wat and faitira.

5. **What are some of the popular animals in Ethiopia?**

    Apart from the black lion, popular animals in Ethiopia are zebras, elephants, gelada monkeys, mountain nyla and the Ethiopian wolf.

6. **What is the name of the popular national park in Ethiopia?**

There are lots of national parks in Ethiopia, but the most popular one is the Simien Mountains National Park.

7. **What is the name of the largest open-air market in all of Africa?**

The largest open-air market in all of Africa is the Mercato Market in Ethiopia.

LOOK OUT FOR MISHA AND
ZIGGY'S NEXT MAGICAL
WILDLIFE ADVENTURE IN . . .

WILD MAGIC

JOURNEY OF THE LOST ELEPHANT

COMING AUGUST 2025

ACKNOWLEDGEMENTS

Wild Magic has been so much fun to write and I'm ecstatic to have my first book for young readers. My guilty pleasure is an animal documentary. I couldn't tell you the amount of times I've watched a series on big cats, or migration, and everything in between. Storytelling about animals always draws me in. Combine that with my obsession with superpowers and now we have *Wild Magic*!

The idea of the black lion came from a picture

of a jet-black lion that went viral on the internet a number of years ago. I was fascinated! When I found out that the image was Photoshopped, I was a little disappointed, but the idea of the black lion stuck in my head. So I explored a bit more and discovered that *real* black lions live in Ethiopia. And so I wanted to write a book that showcased this magical animal in this magnificent country. I want to say a massive thank you to Michelle, Sophia, Yemisrach and Mags for sharing their knowledge of and helping me with my research on Ethiopia. Still in awe that Ethiopia is eight years behind us. Mind-blowing!

I knew I wanted to write a story about superpowered siblings, and then I thought, why not twins? Misha and Ziggy were so much fun to write – they're brave, energetic, love their family and animals and want to protect them. I haven't seen enough Black characters in books sharing their affection, understanding and appreciation for animals and educating readers on why it's important for us to do our part in keeping them safe. Poaching is a massive problem and has led to the unnecessary and immoral deaths of too many animals. If we do not look after them and respect their homes, they will become extinct.

Thank you to my amazing agent, Gemma Cooper, for brainstorming this series with me. I love how excited we both got about the idea of a Black *Wild Thornberrys*! That show is highly underrated. You always have my back and fight for me at every turn. Love you!

Thank you to my editor, Carla, for helping me to bring Misha and Ziggy to life. Thank you to Emma McCann for the brilliant artwork. It's my first time having a heavily illustrated book and I'm so glad that I got to work with you. Thank you to Veronica for your attention to detail and your sweet message about the book. Thank you to Amina for being one of the first people to love the idea of Misha and Ziggy. Lots of love to everyone at Simon & Schuster UK for all your hard work on the book and I can't wait to write more in the series.

Thank you to my family for all of your support. Your prayers continue to open doors for me and I love you all so much – Mum, Lola, Gboli. Hope you're proud up in heaven, Daddy!

Thank you to Anneliese for reading the first

draft. You're such a gem and always make the time to help me. I appreciate you.

I have to mention my beautiful grey Bengal cat and furry bestie, Fergie, who's in this book, but also inspired Yum-Yum in *The Love Dare*. He was my first pet and was the absolute best. He had to be included in my animal book, and I hope he's bothering my dad to play with him up in heaven as much as he bothered me!

Thank you to Ebru for letting me use your dog, Blue, in the book. I hope she's also playing with her toy balls in heaven to her heart's content.

Lastly, thank you to all the readers, the booksellers, the bloggers, librarians and everyone who has championed my books. You are so amazing and I appreciate you all x

ABIOLA BELLO is a Nigerian-British, prize-winning, bestselling children's and YA author who was born and raised in London. She is an advocate for diversity in books for young people. She's the author of the award-winning fantasy series Emily Knight and was nominated for the CILIP's Carnegie Award, won London's BIG Read 2019, and was a finalist for the People's Book Prize Best Children's Book. Abiola contributed to *The Very Merry Murder Club*, a collection of mysteries from thirteen exciting and diverse children's writers which published in October 2021 and was selected as Waterstones Children's Book of the Month. Her debut YA, *Love in Winter Wonderland*, published in November 2022 and was an Amazon's Editor's Choice and was featured in The Guardian's Children's and Teens Best New Novels. Her second YA novel, *Only For The Holidays*, published in October 2023 and was The Bookseller One To Watch, one of Waterstones Best Paperbacks of 2023 and was featured in The Guardian's Children's and Teens Best New Novels. Her third YA novel, *The Love Dare*, was published in July 2024. Abiola won The Black British Business Awards 2023 for Arts and Media and The London Book Fair Trailblazer Awards 2018. She is the co-founder of Hashtag Press, Hashtag BLAK, The Diverse Book Awards and ink!

@ABelloWrites